Berry Woman's Children

by Dale De Armond

Dale DeArmond

Greenwillow Books, New York

First Edition   10 9 8 7 6 5 4 3 2 1

LIBRARY OF CONGRESS
CATALOGING IN PUBLICATION DATA
De Armond, Dale.
Berry Woman's children.
Summary: Brief retellings
of Eskimo animal legends.
1. Eskimos—Alaska—Legends.
2. Indians of North America
—Alaska—Legends.
3. Animals—Folklore.
[1. Eskimos—Legends] I. Title.
E99.E7D345   1985
398.2'08997   84-29760
ISBN O-688-05814-0
ISBN 0-688-05815-9 (lib. bdg.)

Dedicated to
the animals
and birds
who share
the earth
with us

Contents

S it here on the bedplace with me and I'll tell you about the animals, Berry Woman's children.

When Raven made the animals and birds, he told Berry Woman to look after them, and she does to this day. We don't know very much about her, but some say she is very beautiful, and some say she is the moon.

Each animal, each bird has an inua, a soul, like a person. There was a time, long ago, when the birds and animals could take off their feathers or fur and become just like you and me. People and animals and birds could talk to one another. The animals and birds let the hunters kill them so that people could have food and warm clothes. And the people, in the old days, when the long darkness came and the snow was deep, would gather in the kashim to honor the animals who had been killed that year. The dancers put on animal or bird masks and danced to the music of drums, and the singers sang songs about them. The shaman did magic

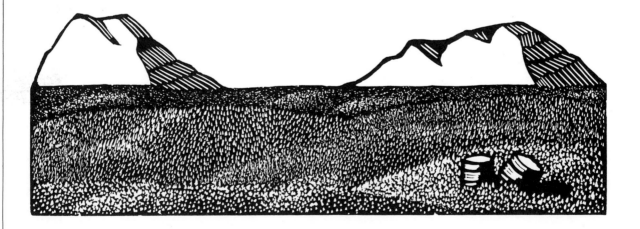

tricks, and sometimes he made a trip to the
moon to ask about the next year's hunting.
At the ceremony's end, each hunter would go
down to the frozen sea, carrying the bladders
of every animal and bird he had killed during
the year. A hole was cut in the ice and the
bladders were dropped into it so that the dead
creatures' inuas were returned to the waters to
become spirits again for other animals.
The old people in the villages still dance to the
music of drums.

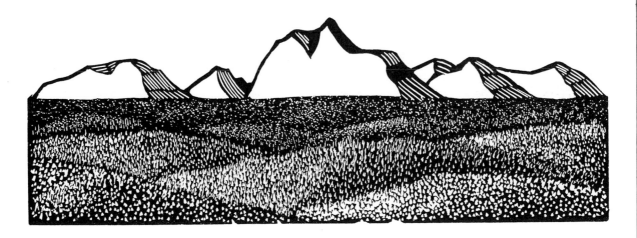

Raven is a very important person. When Raven came, there was only darkness everywhere. So Raven flew around and around, faster and faster and faster, and gathered the darkness into a ball and made the earth. Then Raven made animals and birds. And he found people in beach pea pods.

The walrus return in the spring when the sea ice breaks up. It would be a hungry village without the walrus meat. In the winter the carvers make beautiful carvings of the animals from the walrus tusks. The women split the tough hides to make them thin enough so they can sew them to the frames of the big oomiaks, the hunting boats.

Once when I was a little girl I took my mother's oolu while she was tending the baby. I sharpened it on a beach stone just as I had seen her do and tried to split the hide she was working on and I made a big hole in it. I was afraid and ran away but my mother wasn't angry. She was glad I wanted to learn to split hides and she showed me how to do it. It took me a long time to learn to do it well.

Crab has eyes on stalks and walks sideways on his eight legs. In the winter the village women fish for crabs through a hole in the ice.

There is an old story about a woman who had a crab child. She was so ashamed that she wouldn't let anyone see him. One day her crab child said to her, "Don't hide me away, Mother. Let people see me." So the woman let people see her crab child and he began to look more like a person though he remained a little strange. He became a great hunter and married a girl in the village. They had many children, but none of them were crabs.

Porcupine is round and slow and waddles when he walks. Sometimes he sits in a tree and eats bark and leaves, and sometimes he sits in a tree and just looks at things.

Nobody bothers porcupine because he has sharp quills on his rump and tail, and if you touch them, they stick into you like little fishhooks.

Once there was a very lazy little girl who wouldn't do any work at all. One day she turned into a porcupine and went into the woods and nobody ever saw her again.

A long time ago there were giant eagles. They were so big they caught whales to feed their eaglets. But they all died or were killed, and at last there was just one pair left. They made a nest in a dead volcano. One day the mother eagle carried off a young woman. Her husband was grief-stricken and angry. He was a great hunter and he took his bow and arrows, climbed the volcano, and killed both the giant eagles.

There are no more giant eagles, but eagles still have magic, and we use their down and feathers on our dance sticks.

Sea otter has fur softer than eagle down. When she is hungry, she dives to the bottom of the sea and brings up a rock and a fat sea urchin. She floats on her back and breaks the sea urchin shell on the rock and eats the sweet meat inside.

Sea otter is a very good mother. When her pup is small, she often swims on her back and holds the baby on her chest. She plays games with her child in the water.

The great white bear lives at the edge of the sea. In the winter, when the water freezes, he wanders around on the ice, hunting for seals. Mother polar bear births her cub in an ice cave.

My grandmother told me a scary story about a giant polar bear with ten legs. He could race faster than the wind. All the hunters were afraid of him.

My grandmother said she never saw a ten-legged polar bear.

Little Chief Hare gathers grass all summer long and stores it in his warm burrow under the earth so he will have food in the winter.

A woman from a distant village told me a story about Little Chief Hare. Once long ago, when spring came, there was no game and it was a very hungry time in her village. The people asked Little Chief Hare what to do. He called all the villagers together and led them to a mountain. Then he told them to sing very loud. The villagers did this and soon a great door opened in the mountain. All the animals came tumbling out and ran off. There was lots of game for the hunters and no one was hungry anymore.

In the spring the men in the village keep a whale watch. When they sight a whale, the whaling captains and their crews run to put the big oomiaks in the water and go after the whales. When a boat comes back towing a whale, all the villagers come down to help bring the whale ashore and cut it up. Everybody shares in the good meat and the rich white muktuk, the blubber that keeps the whale warm in the cold waters of the sea. Once Raven flew into a whale's mouth and down his throat. He found himself in a big room lit by an oil lamp. The whale's inua made Raven welcome and he stayed in the whale for four days. But Raven was greedy and he ate parts of the whale, and the whale died and floated ashore. Some people from a nearby village found the whale and cut it up, and that's how Raven was able to escape.

Puffin burrows into the side of a cliff to make her nest. Her wings are very short, and when she wants to fly, she jumps off the cliff and flaps her wings very hard, and just before she hits the water she finally flies.

Once a shaman was out hunting. He struck a puffin with his spear, and just as the puffin died, the shaman saw the puffin's inua come out of its mouth. The shaman went home and carved a mask of the puffin and its inua and made up a dance about it. He wore the mask when he danced. This pleased the puffin's inua very much.

Grizzly bear is very big and fierce and only the bravest hunters dare to hunt him.

I heard a story about a young woman who laughed at a bear and the bear people carried her off. She married one of the bears and their children were half bear and half human. One day the woman brought her children home to her village, but the children were very wild and fierce so they went back to live with the bears.

Loon nests close to a lake. Mother and father loon take turns sitting on the eggs to keep them warm. When the eggs hatch, both parents watch over the chicks and teach them to fly and to dive deep into the water.

Loon has a strange night song. Once a loon dived and sang with a blind boy until his eyes were healed and he could see. He was so grateful that he gave loon a necklace which she still wears.

Seal spends most of his time in the water and is a fast swimmer. In the winter he makes a breathing hole in the sea ice.

The hunters like to wear sealskin pants when they go out in the big oomiaks so they will stay warm and dry.

My grandfather once brought me an orphan baby seal. He made noises like a baby and he liked to be held like a baby. He followed me everywhere. When he got big, I took him back to the sea. For a long time he came back to play with me. But one day he went off with other seals and I never saw him again.

The wild geese come in the spring to make their nests and raise their young on the tundra. All summer long the families live together, and when the cranberries are ripe in the fall, they all fly south.

Once Raven fell in love with a beautiful young goose and married her. When it was time to fly south, he found he couldn't keep up with the geese even though his wife tried to help him. At last she had to fly away with the others, leaving poor Raven behind.

Tumble into bed now, little ones, and dream of Berry Woman and her animals and birds. Always remember to give them honor and respect for all they give us. Then the inuas will be content and the village will be a happy place. Soon it will be the time of the winter dances. The men are making new covers for the drums. We will go to the kashim and people will do the old dances. I will wear my dance gloves and the Berry Woman mask, and dance for her.

Glossary and Pronounciation Guide

ANNA (AH-na). Grandmother.

INUA (ee-NEW-ah). Spirit or soul. Each living thing or natural object has an inua which can take on other physical forms.

KASHIM (or kassim)   (ka-SHEEM). Meeting place.

MUKTUK (or maktak)   (MUCK-tuck). Whale skin with blubber (layer of fat). A favorite delicacy in a land where the body requires large amounts of fat to survive the cold.

OOLU (OO-loo). Woman's knife. A crescent-shaped knife with an ivory or bone handle, used for splitting walrus hides, skinning animals, cleaning fish, etc.

OOMIAK (OO-mee-ack). A large skin boat used for hunting and transportation.

SHAMAN (SHAW-man). Medicine man or witch doctor, conjurer.